CITYVIEW SCHOOL
MATERIALS PURCHASED
W/READING 1ST GRANT

Schultz

THIS BOOK BELONGS TO:

Hissss!

Mick Inkpen

Red Wagon Books

Harcourt, Inc.

San Diego   New York   London

T he sun was making
a shadow of Kipper
on the wall.
It was a hot day.
A very hot day.

Kipper lay on his blanket and sucked his drink through a curly-wurly straw.

"Today is a wading pool kind of day," he said.

The wading pool was on the top shelf of the toy closet.

Kipper grabbed it and pulled enthusiastically.

The toys in the closet fell on Kipper's head.

Ouch!

It was hard work blowing up the wading pool.

So when Kipper was finished, he turned on the hose and went to buy an ice-cream cone.

On the way back,
the ice cream
melted down Kipper's
paw and plopped into
a puddle.

"That's odd," said
Kipper. "It wasn't
raining when I left."

The puddle was as big as a pond. In the middle was Kipper's wading pool, looking very saggy.

"I know what has happened," said Kipper.

Kipper knelt down and listened very carefully to the wading pool.

With his big ears he could just hear a tiny,

tiny

hissssssssssssssssssssssssssss

SSSSSSSSS!

Kipper took the
Band-Aid from
his head.

Ouch!

And he mended the
wading pool...

…which was clever,

wasn't it?

Library of Congress Cataloging-in-Publication Data
Inkpen, Mick.
Hissss!/by Mick Inkpen.
p.   cm.
"Red Wagon Books."
Summary: On a hot summer day when Kipper the dog discovers
a leak in his wading pool, he fixes it in a very unusual way.
[1. Dogs—Fiction.   2. Summer—Fiction.]   I. Title.
PZ7.I564Hi   2000
[E]—dc21   99-6728
ISBN 0-15-202415-8

A C E F D B

Printed in Hong Kong